AF480711

I

Copyright @ Keenan Dailey 2020

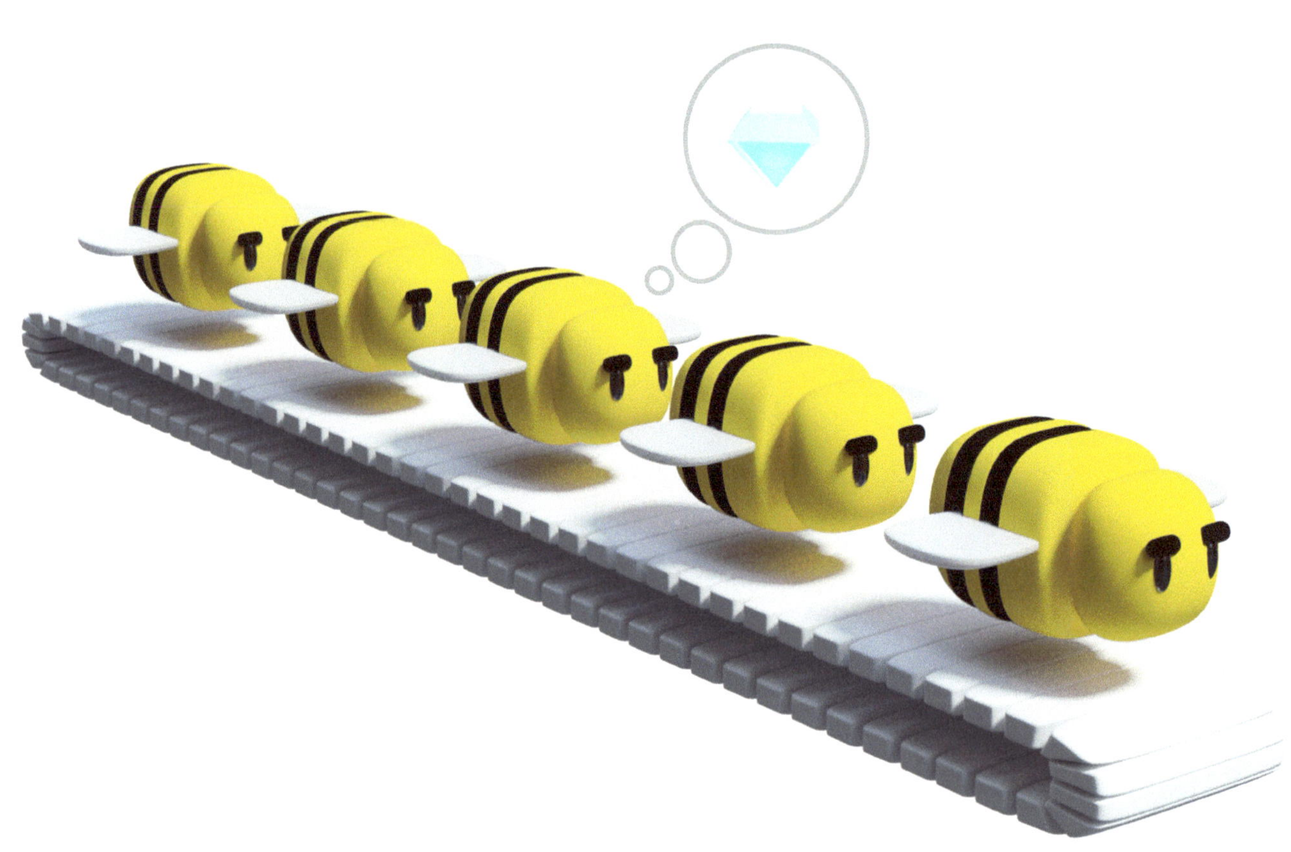

"You all need to improve your communication
It's dangerous to go alone! Take this."

愚蠢的蜜蜂

PUFF

I made Puff so that I can make money.

Making art can be really fulfilling but
you gotta pay them bills

Book 2 depends on the bills.

instagram.com/keenanedailey

www.ingramcontent.com/pod-product-compliance
Lightning Source LLC
Chambersburg PA
CBHW042130110726
48006CB00003B/827